ODD ONE OUT

Penguin Workshop
An Imprint of Penguin Random House

PENGUIN WORKSHOP
Penguin Young Readers Group
An Imprint of Penguin Random House LLC

Copyright © 2018 by Buster Books. All rights reserved. First published in Great Britain in 2018 by Buster Books, an imprint of Michael O'Mara Books Limited. Published in the United States in 2018 by Penguin Workshop, an imprint of Penguin Random House LLC, 345 Hudson Street, New York, New York 10014. PENGUIN and PENGUIN WORKSHOP are trademarks of Penguin Books Ltd, and the W colophon is a trademark of Penguin Random House LLC. Manufactured in China.

Designed by Derrian Bradder

With material adapted from www.shutterstock.com

ISBN 9781524790882   10 9 8 7 6 5 4 3 2 1

How to use this book

Simply pick a puzzle and follow the instructions on the left-hand page. Whether you're finding an odd one out, matching pairs, or spotting specific emoticons, there's plenty to keep your brain bamboozled on every page, along with fun facts to keep you entertained. If you get stuck, all the answers are at the back of the book.

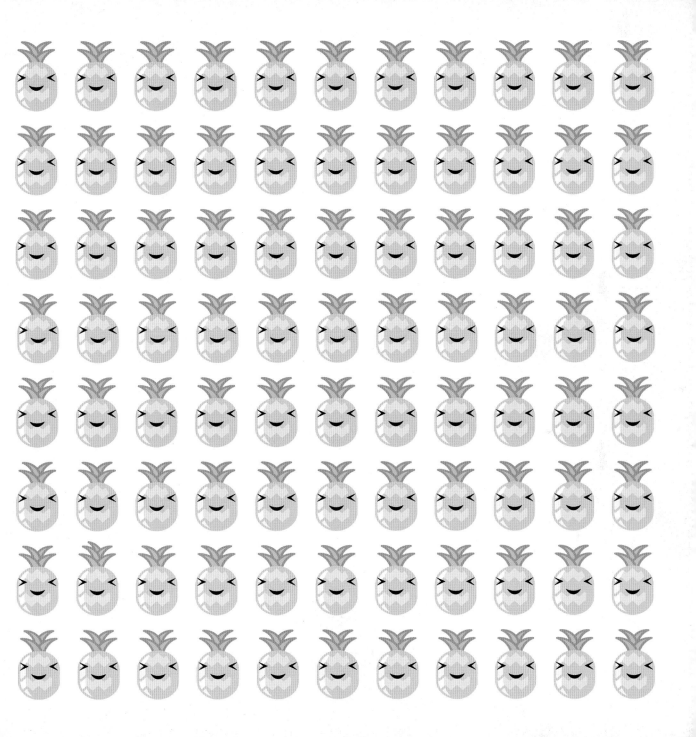

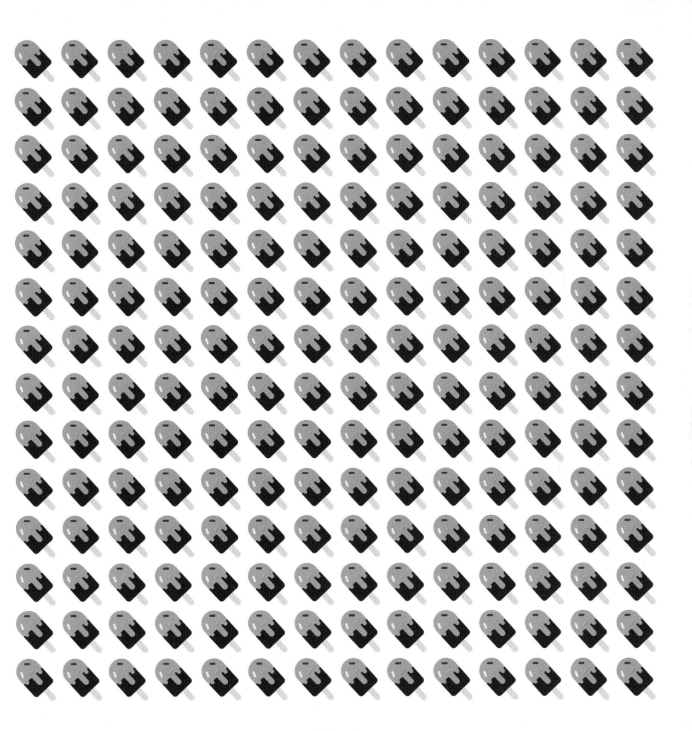

Every bottle has
an identical buddy.
Pair them all up.

The human body contains
around 60 chemical elements.

Strawberries are technically not a fruit. What look like tiny seeds on their skin are actually the fruit, and inside each fruit is an even tinier seed.

Find these four faces:

The tiger is the largest species of the cat family.

Find two odd pairs.

The spines of cacti have been used in the production of hooks, combs, and needles.

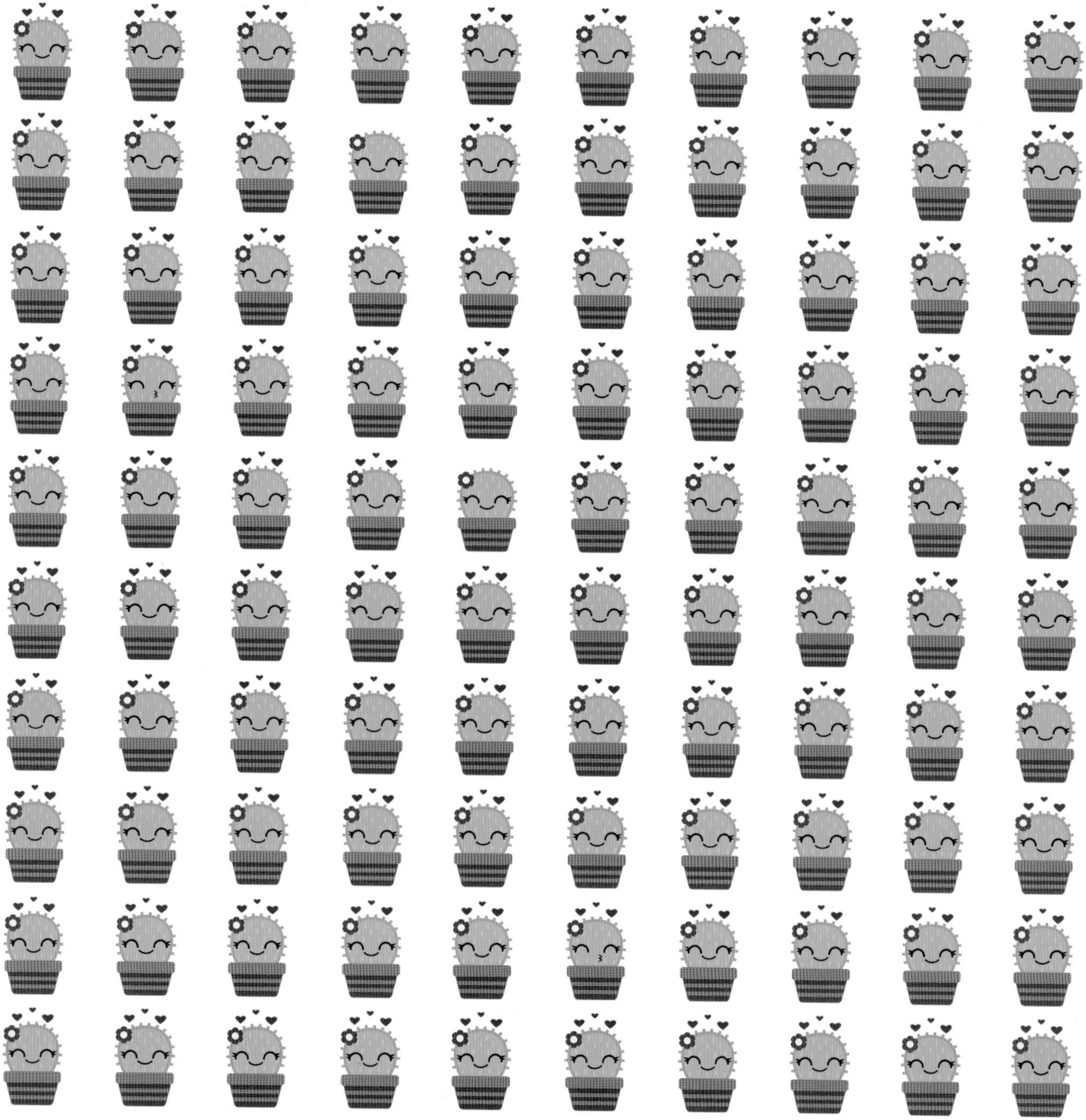

Find these six cupcakes:

Before sophisticated decorating equipment came along, people used feathers to spread icing on cakes.

Find one odd pair.

There are more than 2,500 varieties of apples grown in the United States.

Which plant is the largest?

Researchers have found that plants can recognize family and will compete less for root space with their plant family members than when surrounded by plants that are different.

Humans are born with a preference
for things that taste sweet.

Find one odd pair.

With every passing century, the length of the day on Earth increases by nearly two milliseconds as the planet's rotation gradually slows down.

Spot two odd ones out.

One theory tells us that the black mask around a raccoon's eyes deflects glare, which helps with its night vision.

Find this face:

It has been suggested that the same part of the brain is responsible for both crying and laughing, perhaps explaining why they sometimes occur together.

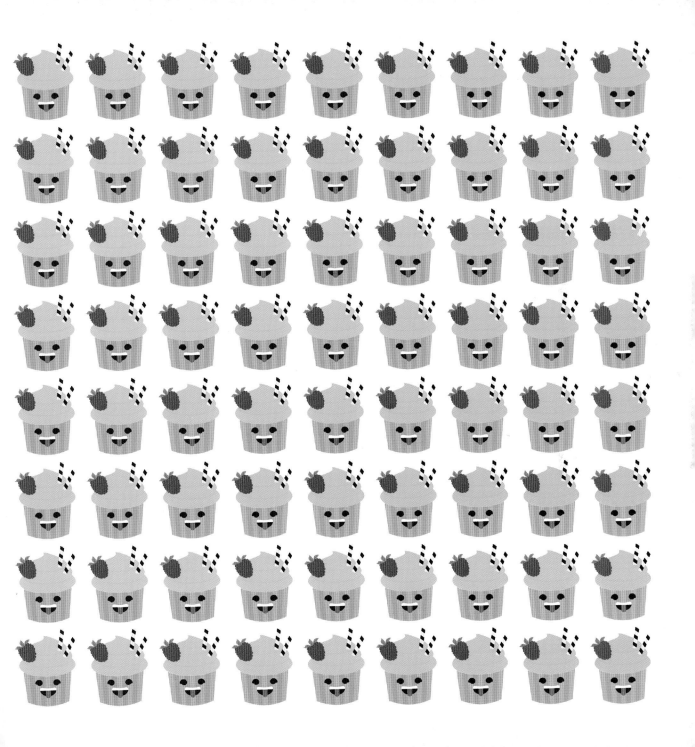

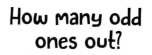

How many odd ones out?

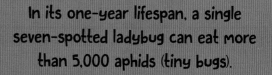

In its one-year lifespan, a single seven-spotted ladybug can eat more than 5,000 aphids (tiny bugs).

Spinning pizza dough has its own sporting event at the World Pizza Championship. Pizza teams compete in acrobatic dough-spinning competitions.

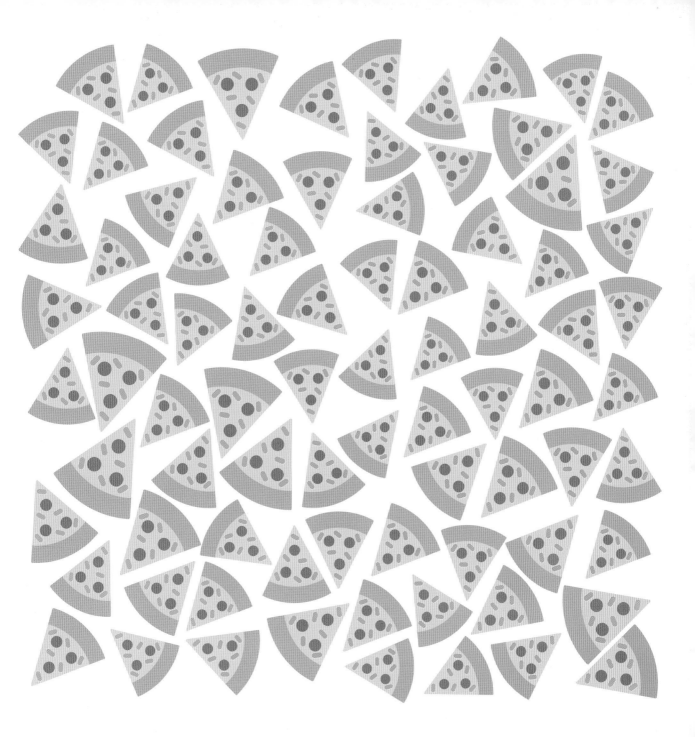

Every alien has
an identical buddy.
Pair them all up.

The Drake Equation is a mathematical
calculation that estimates the number
of possible extraterrestrial civilizations
in the Milky Way Galaxy.

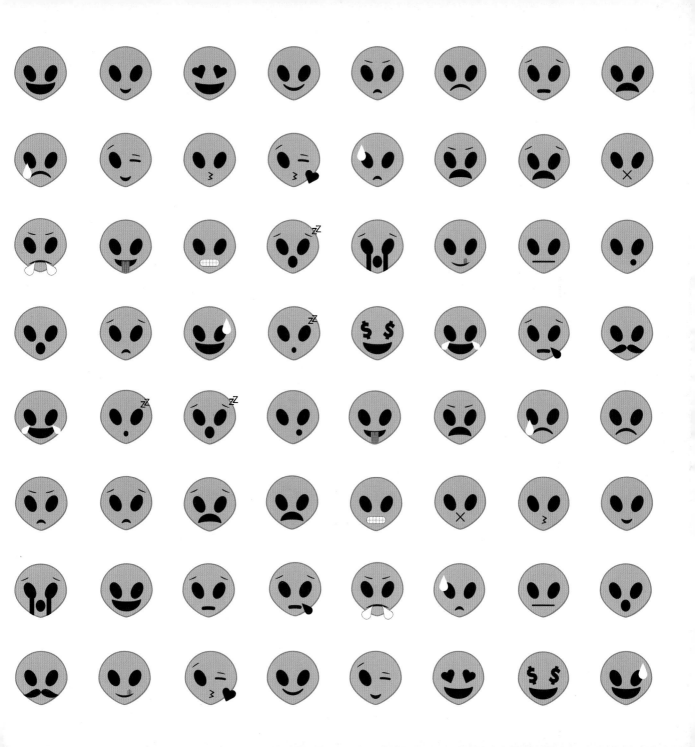

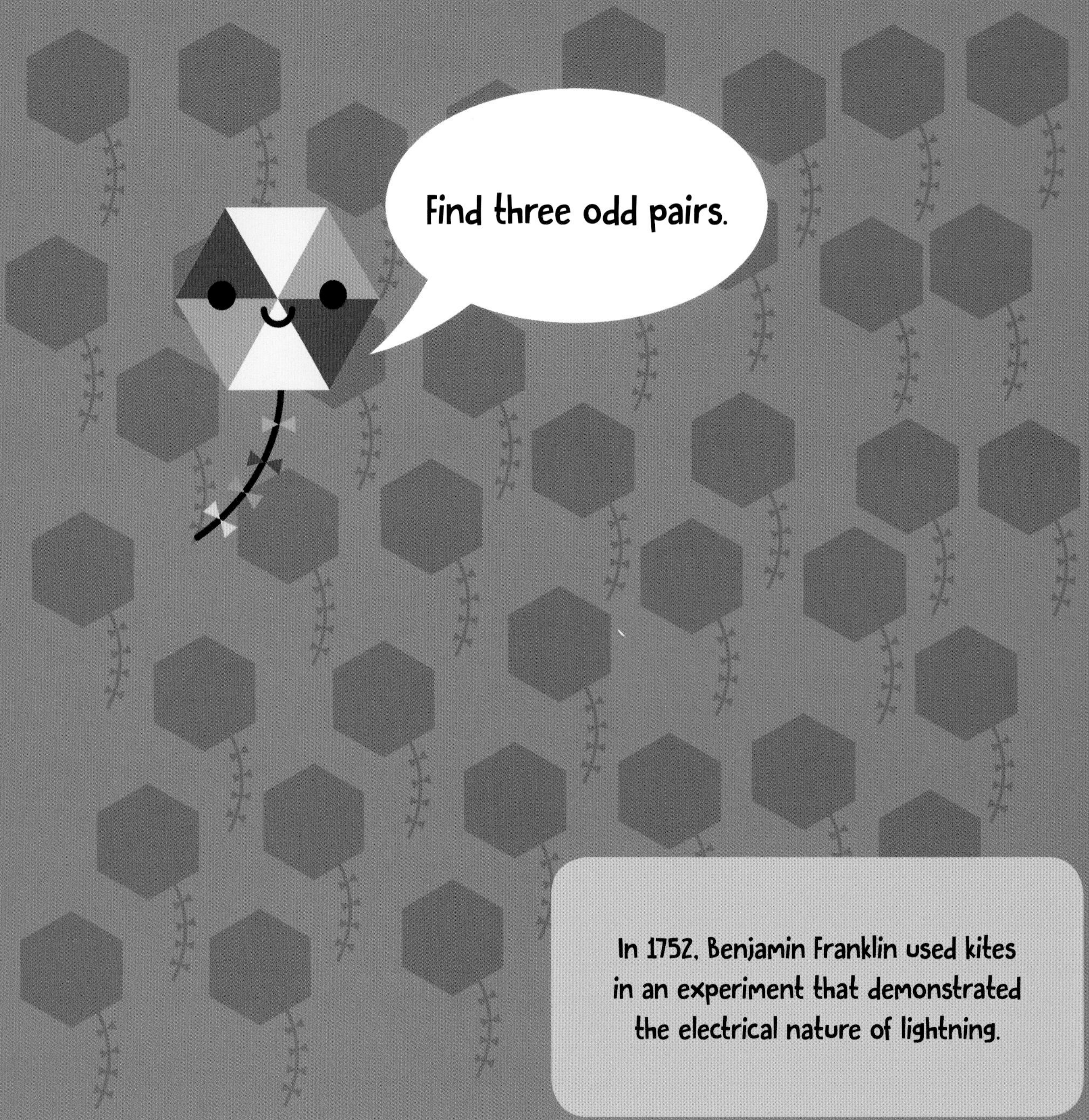

In 1752, Benjamin Franklin used kites in an experiment that demonstrated the electrical nature of lightning.

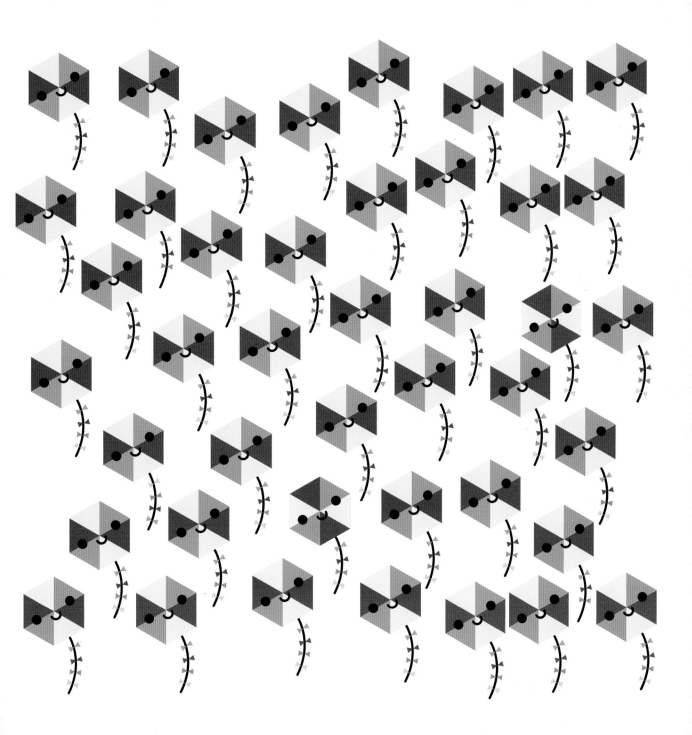

Researchers have found that simply being told you are blushing, even when you're not, is enough to make you blush.

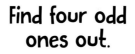

Find four odd
ones out.

Dogs can recognize over 150 words.

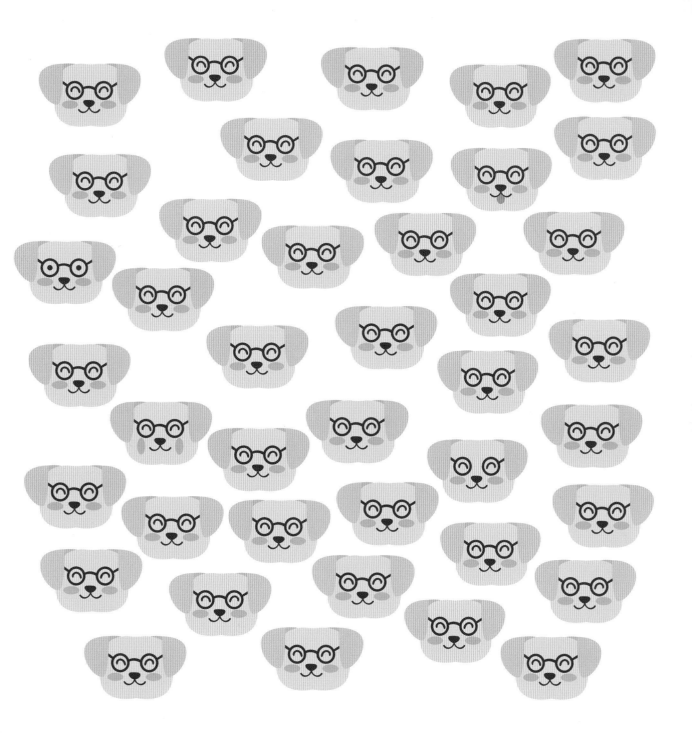

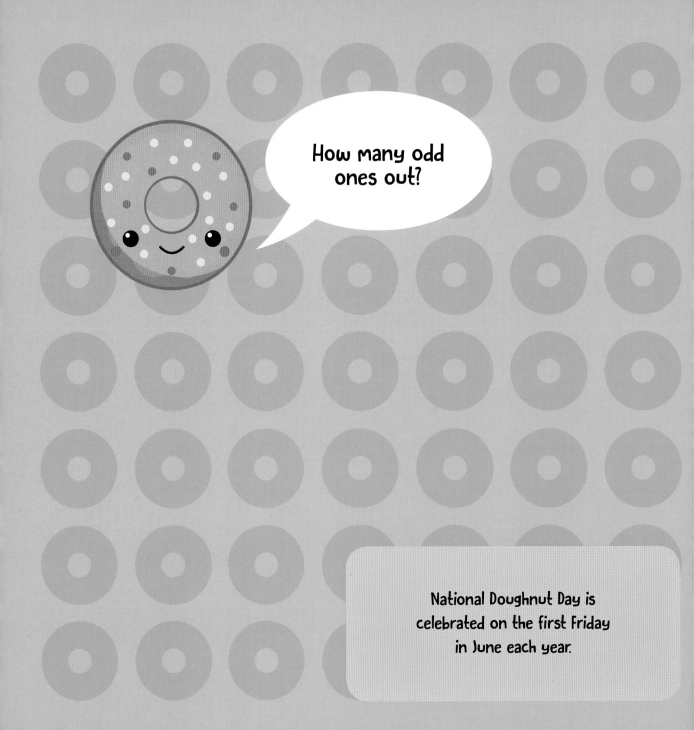

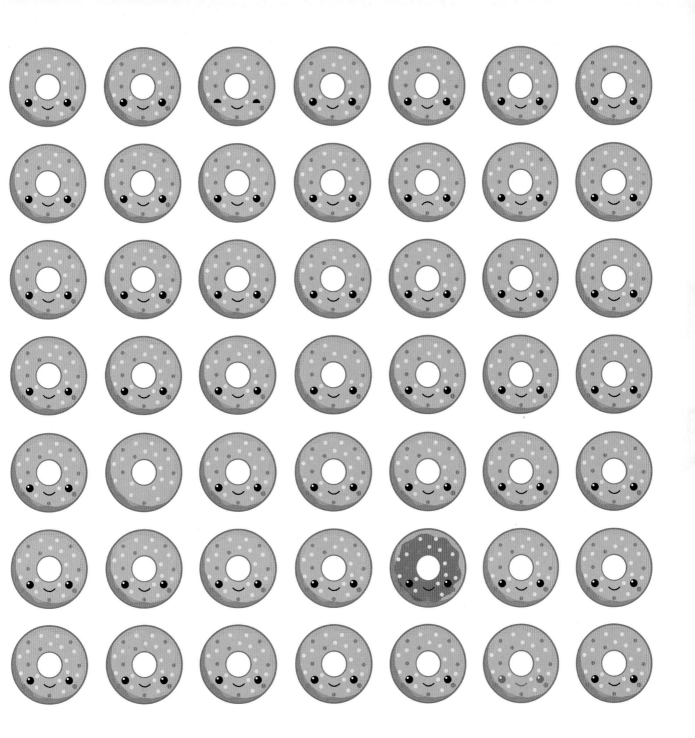

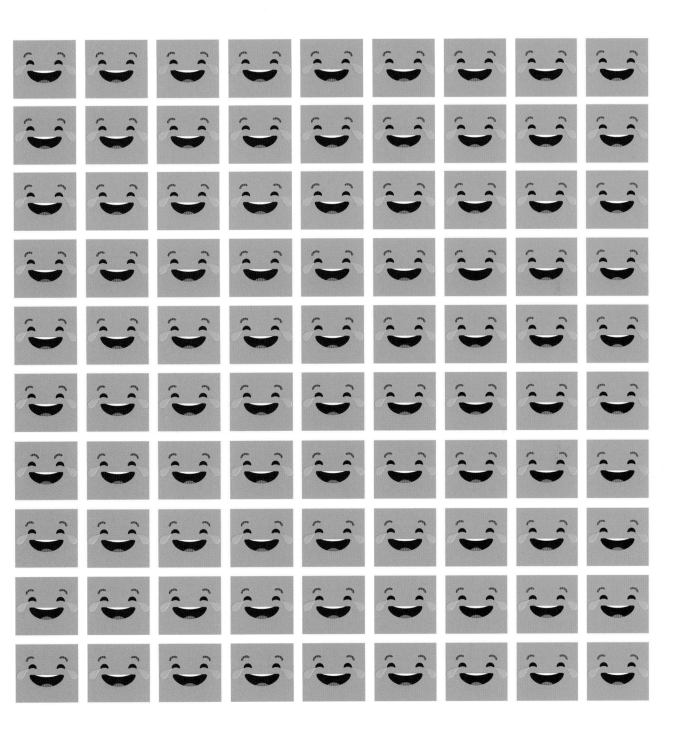

Find three odd pairs.

The smell of real Christmas trees came eighth in a survey of people's favorite smells, just behind the sea but ahead of perfume.

Find four odd pairs.

The largest pumpkin pie ever was baked in 2010. It weighed 3,699 pounds and had a diameter of 20 feet.

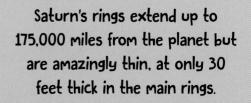

How many odd ones out?

Saturn's rings extend up to 175,000 miles from the planet but are amazingly thin, at only 30 feet thick in the main rings.

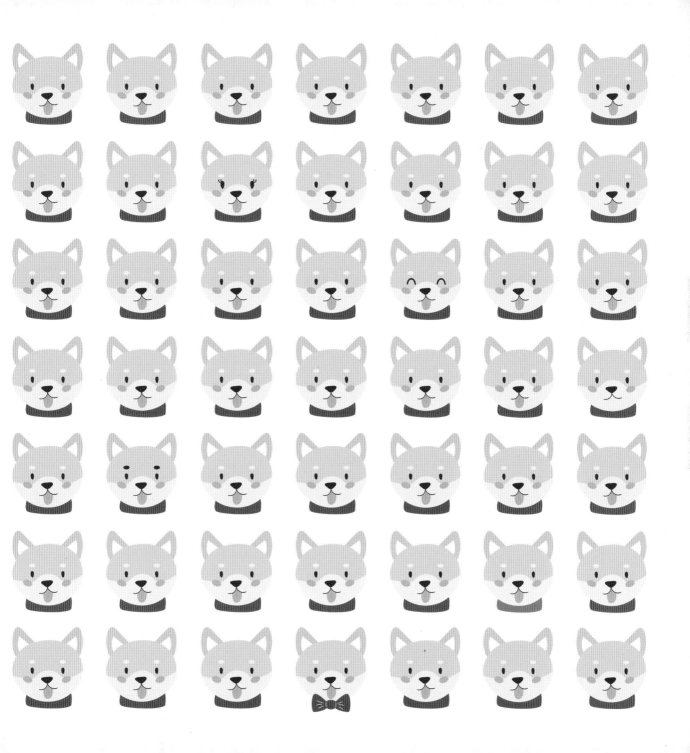

Spot five odd ones out.

Depending on the species, cacti can survive for 15 to 300 years.

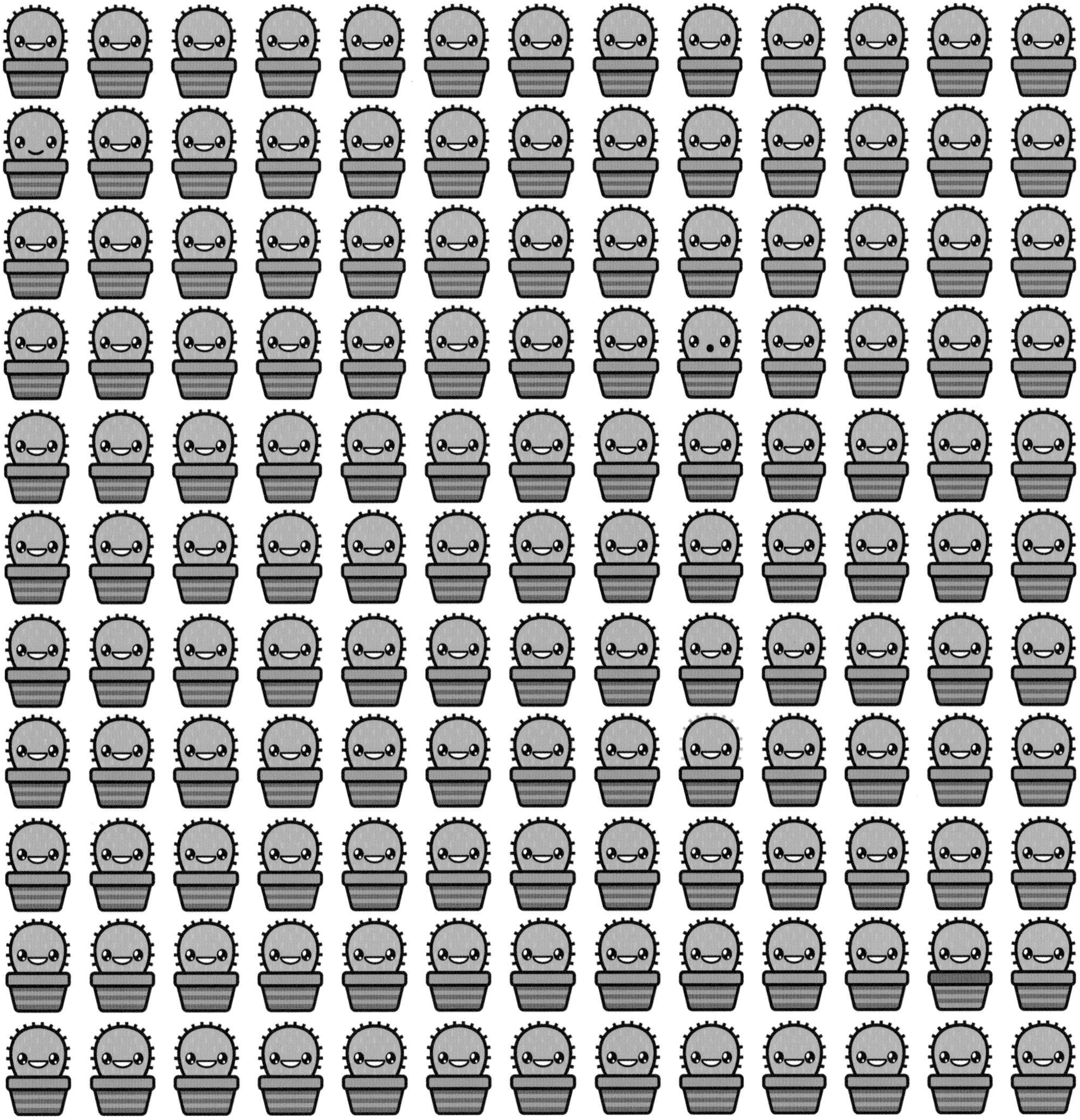

Every car has an identical buddy. Pair them all up.

In 1886, Carl Benz built an automobile called the Benz Patent-Motorwagen. This is considered to be the first modern car.

Spot three odd ones out.

Pittsburgh's Monroeville Mall was the location of George Romero's classic zombie film *Dawn of the Dead.*

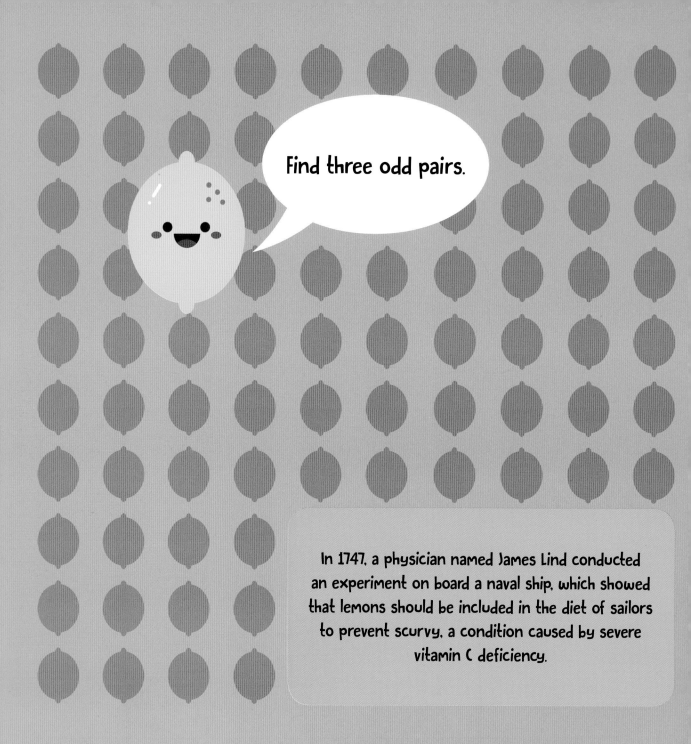

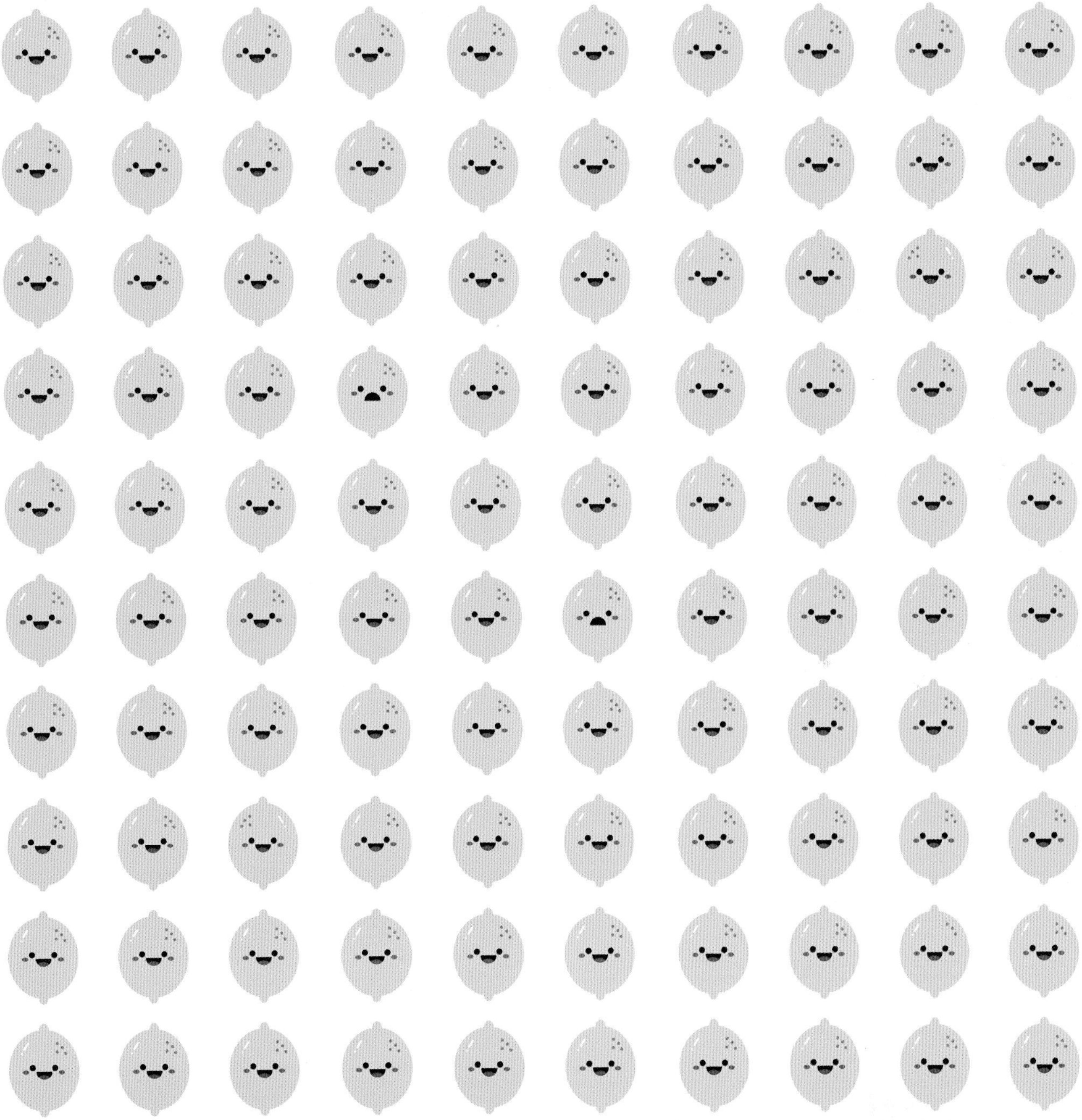

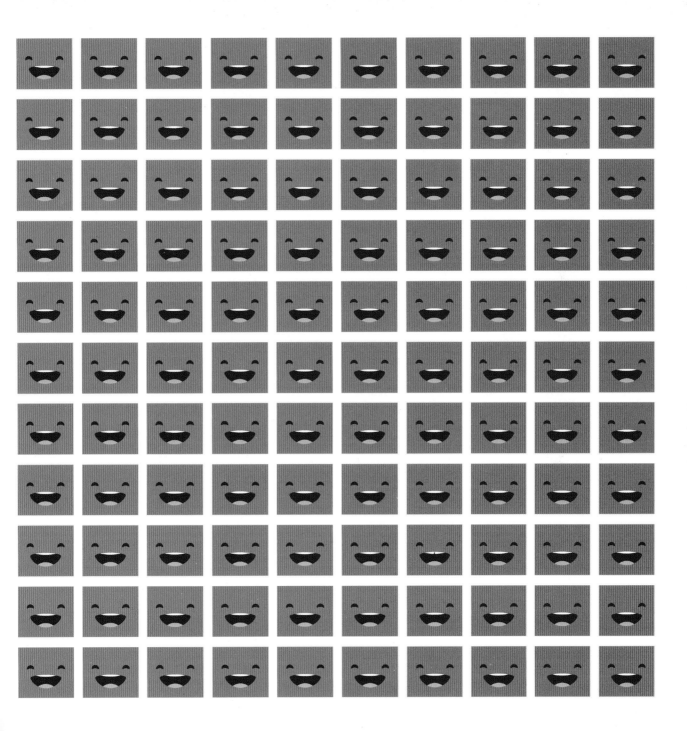

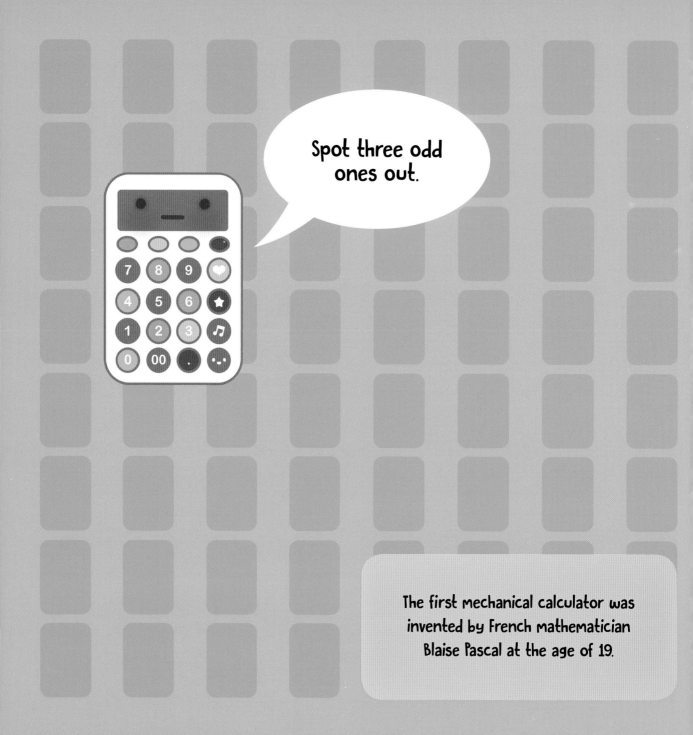

The first mechanical calculator was invented by French mathematician Blaise Pascal at the age of 19.

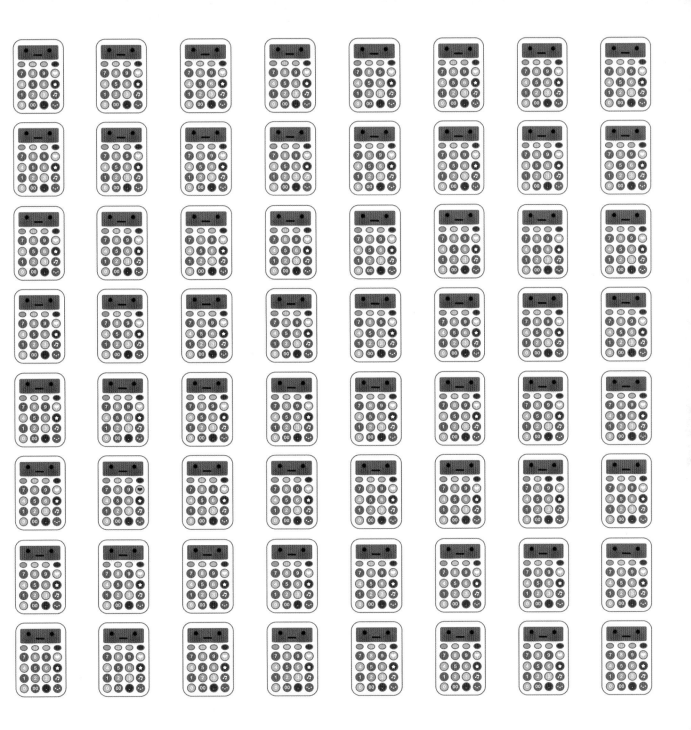

Find five pairs.

A sunflower's head is made of many tiny flowers called florets.

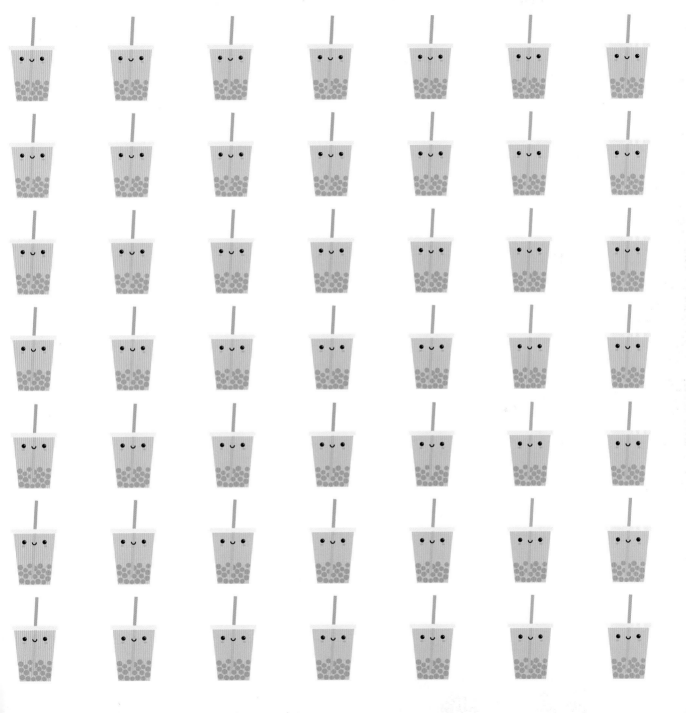

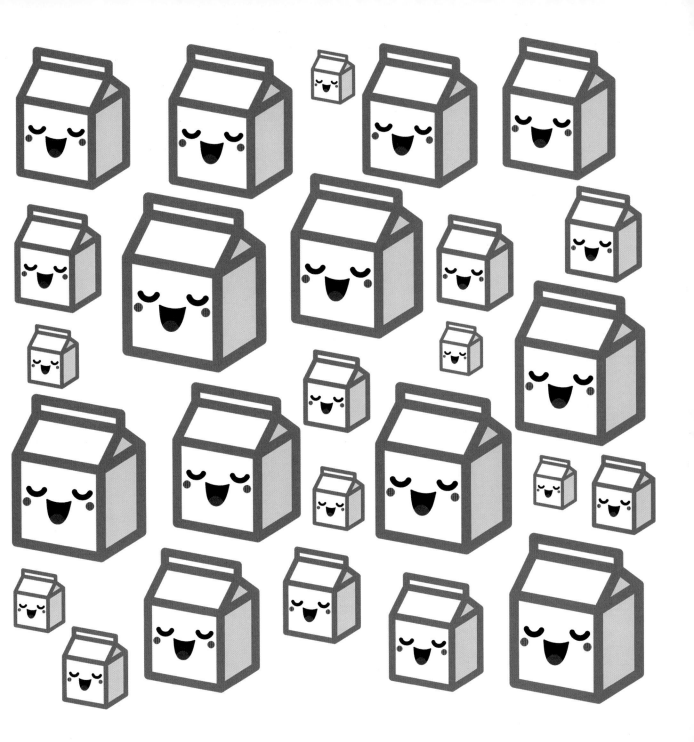

Spot four odd ones out.

This type of plant is called a succulent. "Succulent" comes from the Latin word *sucus*, meaning juice or sap.

The color of a star can range from red to white to blue, and indicates its temperature. Red is the coolest color and blue is the hottest.

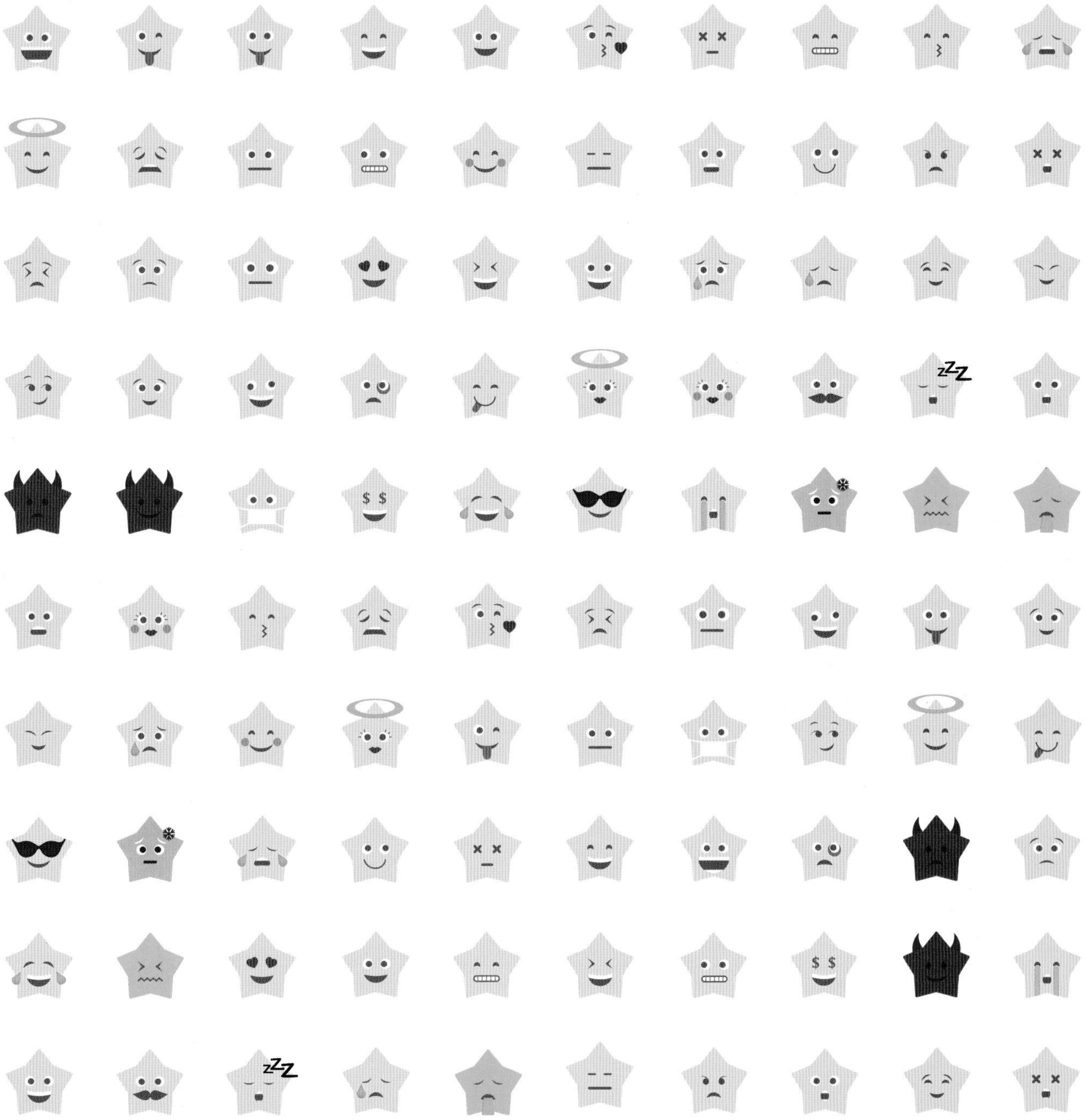

All the Answers

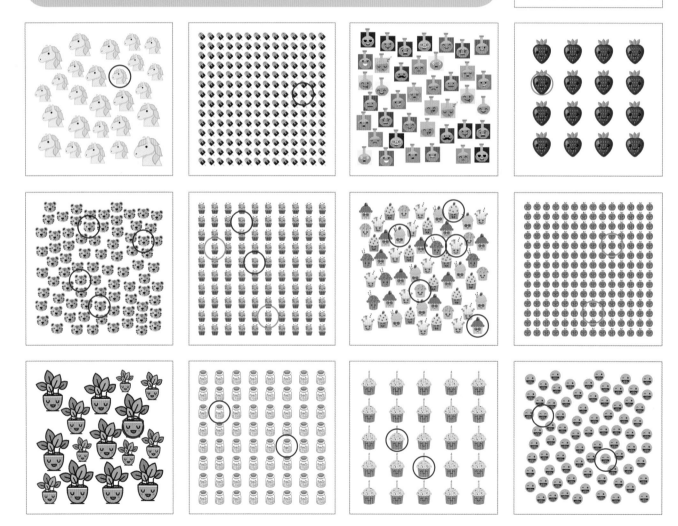

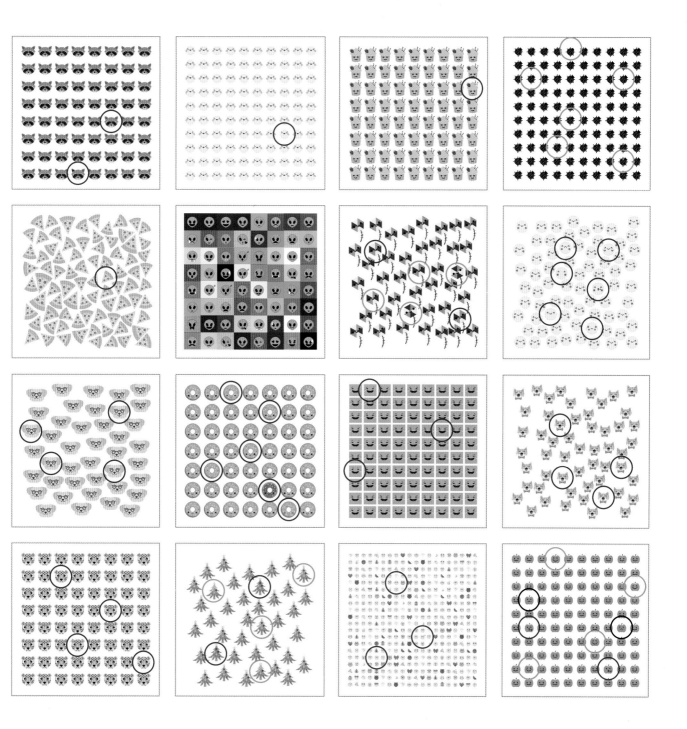

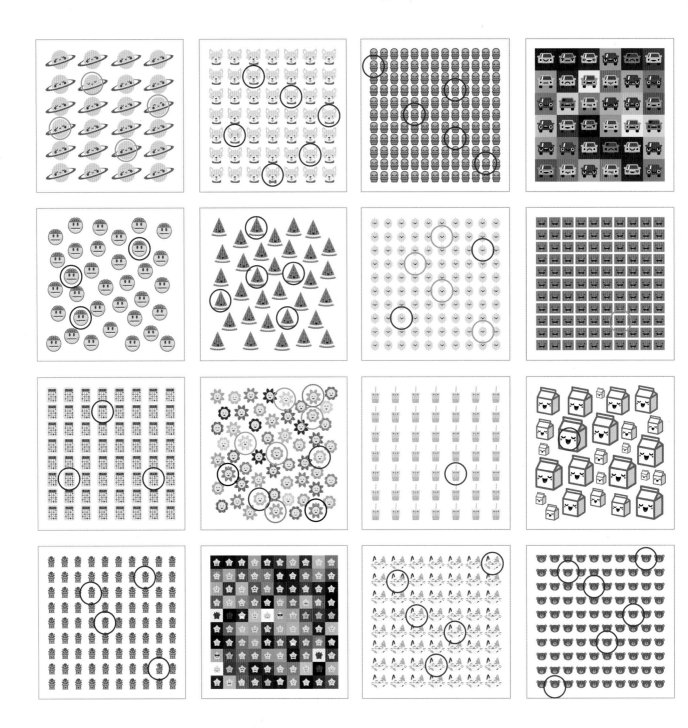